THIS WALKER BOOK BELONGS TO:

_____

_____

_____

pulling

balancing

measuring

teaching

hiding

sliding

cooking

tasting

throwing

pointing

stretching

tickling

finding

hiding

climbing

standing

marching

waiting

For Alice

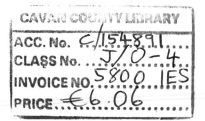
First published 1994 by Walker Books Ltd
87 Vauxhall Walk, London SE11 5HJ

This edition published 2004

2 4 6 8 10 9 7 5 3 1

This book has been typeset in Plantin

Printed in China

British Library Cataloguing in Publication Data:
a catalogue record for this book is available from the British Library

ISBN 1-84428-471-9

www.walkerbooks.co.uk

Hiding

Shirley Hughes

WALKER BOOKS
AND SUBSIDIARIES
LONDON · BOSTON · SYDNEY · AUCKLAND

You can't see me, I'm hiding!

Here I am.

I'm hiding again!

Bet you can't find me this time!

Under a bush in the garden
is a very good place to hide.

So is a big
umbrella,

or down at the end
of the bed.

Sometimes Dad hides behind a newspaper.

And Mum hides behind a book on the sofa.

You can even hide under a hat.

Tortoises hide inside their shells
when they aren't feeling friendly,

and hamsters hide right at the
back of their cages when they
want to go to sleep.

When the baby hides his eyes
he thinks you can't see him.
But he's there all the time!

A lot of things seem to hide –
the moon behind the clouds,

and the sun behind the trees.

Flowers need to hide in the ground
in wintertime.

But they come peeping out again
in the spring.

Buster always hides when it's time
for his bath,

and so does Mum's purse when we're
all ready to go out shopping.

Our favourite place to hide is behind the kitchen door. Then we jump out – BOO!

And can you guess
who's hiding behind
these curtains?

You're right!
Now we're coming out –
is everyone clapping?

pulling

balancing

measuring

teaching

hiding

sliding

cooking

tasting

throwing

pointing

stretching

tickling

finding

hiding

climbing

standing

marching

waiting

WALKER BOOKS is the world's leading

independent publisher of children's books.

Working with the best authors and illustrators

we create books for all ages, from babies

to teenagers – books your child will

grow up with and always remember. So…

FOR THE BEST CHILDREN'S BOOKS,
LOOK FOR THE BEAR